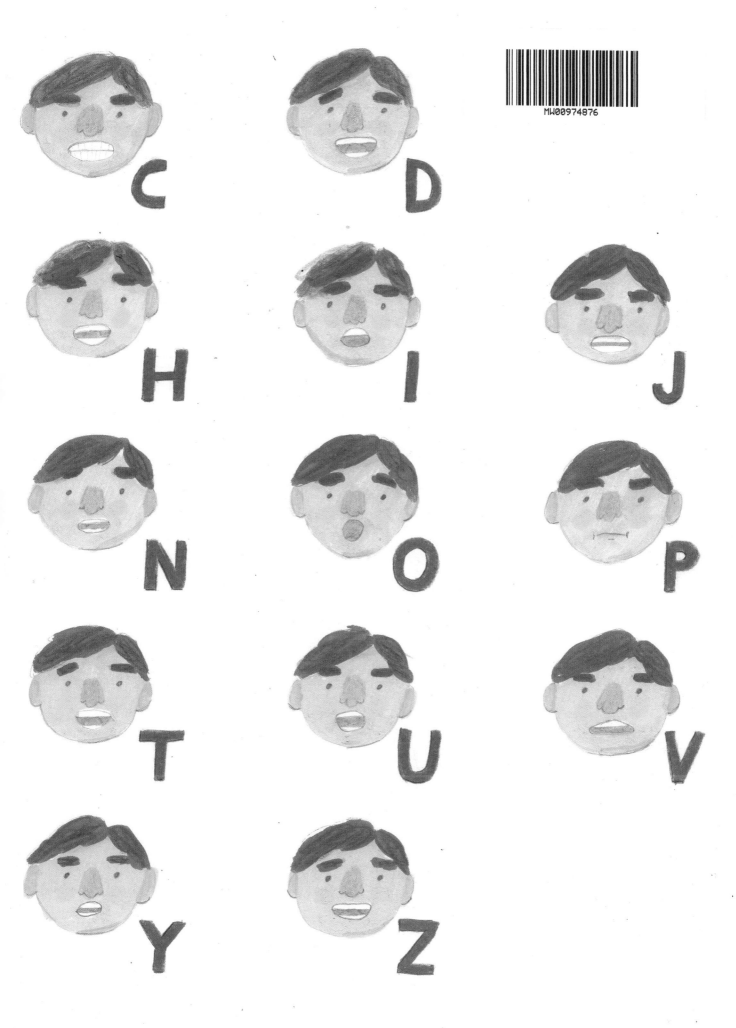

How to Teach
a Troll to Read

To-Kylie, Emma,
+ Gibson,

Read Happy!
Kelly Stucky
21 Oct. 2023

Author Kelly Stuckey was born and raised in Arkansas, but after living in the Atlanta area for twenty-five years, she considers herself a Georgia peach. She has a B.A. in Literature and Art History and is trained in Orton-Gillingham reading instruction. She enjoys going on adventures with her husband and children, playing with her dogs, and any creative problem that needs solving. "How to Teach a Troll to Read" is Kelly's first children's book.

Illustrator Kristiana Dorosconoka is from Riga, Latvia, and is currently living in the countryside in the United Kingdom. She has an M.A. in Children's Picturebook Illustration from the Cambridge School of Art. Kristiana loves to draw pictures in the fields, and being close to nature inspires her art.

Library of Congress Control Number: 2022904033
ISBN: 978-1-7378420-0-2
Printed in the United States of America
Illustrations by Kristiana Dorosconoka
Book Design by Rachel Martin
This book is printed in Open Dyslexic Font

How to Teach
a Troll to Read

Written by
Kelly Stuckey
Illustrated by
Kristiana Dorosconoka

Once upon a time,
there was a Troll who
lived under a bridge. He was grouchy
and irritable,
hairy and scary.

Worst of all,
he had **stinky feet**.

But he had not always been a Troll. He used to be a boy named Tom, who lived with his grandmother and a dog named **Natty**.

His grandmother loved to sit by the
window in a comfy chair and read.

On the first day of school,
Tom hopped on the big yellow
bus and took the long,

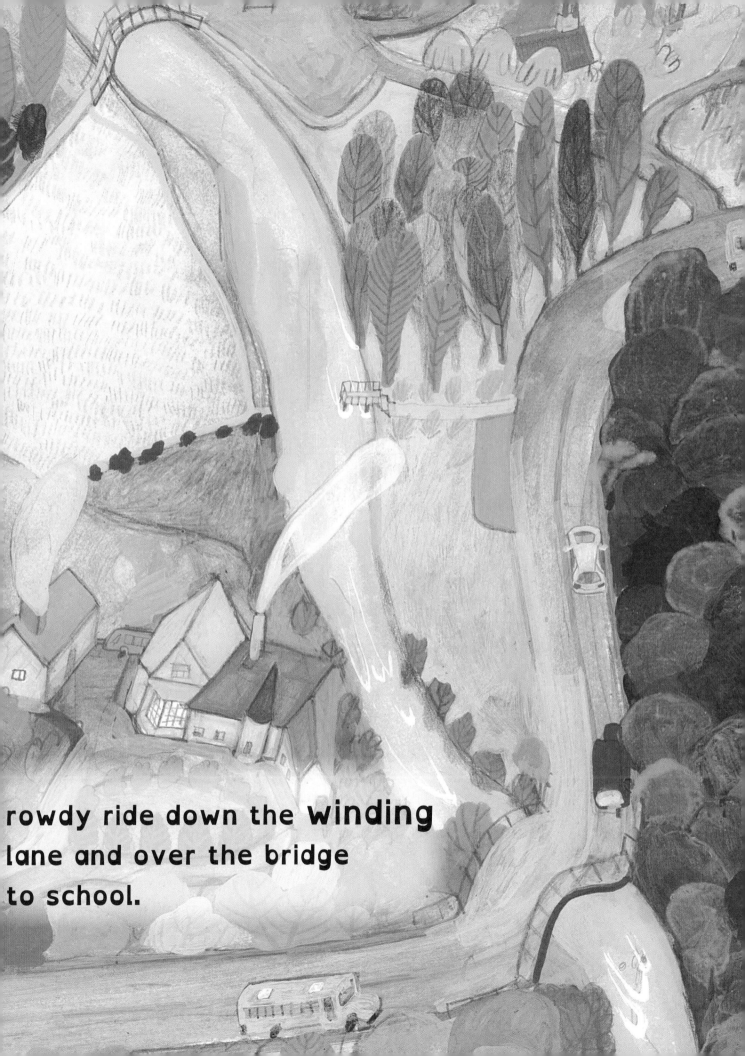

rowdy ride down the **winding** lane and over the bridge to school.

He got **compliments** from his music teacher,

and he was the **first** one finished with the math quiz.

But when it was Tom's turn to read, he got the letters mixed up in his head.

He kept making mistakes,
and the kids started to laugh.

Then, when he slipped off his shoes
to get more comfortable, the kids called him
"Stupid Stinky Feet."

Tom shouted back, "I am not stupid!"

That afternoon Natty was waiting for Tom at the bus stop.

He walked up to pet her, but as soon as he got close,

Natty saw a rabbit and started to chase it.

Tom followed as fast as he could, but soon he lost sight of Natty.

He sat down under the bridge to think and fell fast asleep.

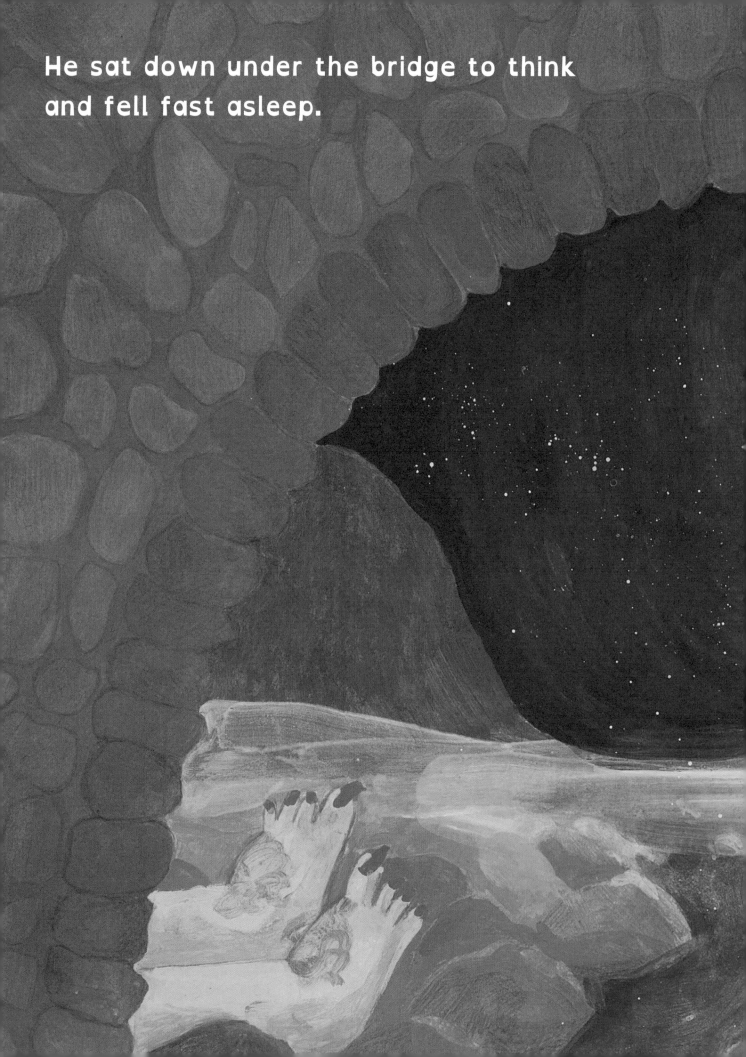

Then, at midnight,
a rare **lunar eclipse** occurred.

Everything went completely dark, and a frosty
mist fell over the bridge.

When Tom woke up
the next morning,
he was **hairy**.
His hands were larger.

His feet were huge, and they stunk
worse than ever.

Every morning, the kids hopped on the bus

and took the long, rowdy ride down the winding

lane and over the bridge to school.

The rumble woke the Troll.
He shook the bridge in **anger**.

A girl on the bus named Meg was **curious** about the shaking bridge. That afternoon, she skipped the bus and ran home.

Meg crept down under the bridge, sat on a rock, and pulled out her phonics book to work on a lesson.

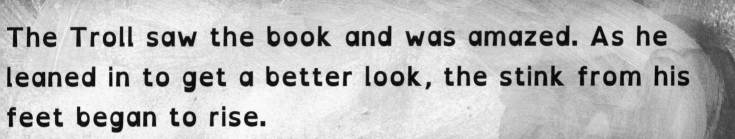

The Troll saw the book and was amazed. As he leaned in to get a better look, the stink from his feet began to rise.

When Meg got a whiff of Troll feet, she dropped the book and **fled**.

The Troll **marveled** at the book and took it to his bed of moss and leaves. He wanted to study it more closely.

Later, Meg went back to the bridge to find her book.

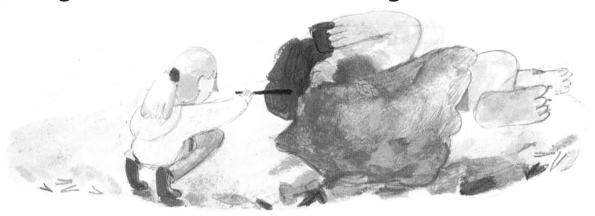

She poked at a pile of leaves in the corner.

The Troll stood up
and let out a loud roar.

Meg said, "Give me my book."
The Troll said, **"NOOO!"**

"I'll trade you
a cookie
for it," she said.

"My name is Meg. I can teach you to read," she said.

The Troll said, "OK."

"Carve the letters and practice the sound each one makes every day," she said.

The Troll said, "I promise
to practice every day."
"Then I promise to come back and
teach you more lessons," Meg said.

Once they had completed all the lessons and he could read, the Troll was immensely proud.

He danced and sang all evening with his forest animal friends

and went happily to sleep.

Later, at midnight, a **rare** lunar eclipse occurred. Everything went dark, and a frosty mist fell over the bridge.

When Tom woke up, he was not a Troll anymore. He was a bit larger and hairier, but he did not mind.

Tom walked home. His grandmother was in the chair. He began to read over her shoulder. "Once upon a time, there was a Troll who lived under a bridge."

His Grandmother said, "Tom, I am glad you came out of your room. I have a book I think you would like. It is about a **Troll.**"

This book is dedicated to
My mother Nancy
who taught me to read.